A Dime Today
A Dollar Tomorrow

Learning to Build Lasting Wealth

*Teaching your child how to build lasting wealth
from a Christian perspective*

Trupac Christian Books

1ˢᵗ Edition

BY ROSS HAYNES JR.

Copyright © 2016 by Ross Haynes Jr. 729670
ISBN: Softcover   978-1-5144-5361-2
        Hardcover   978-1-5144-5362-9
        EBook   978-1-5144-5360-5

This is a work of fiction. Names, characters,
places and incidents either are the product of the
author's imagination or are used fictitiously, and any
resemblance to any actual persons, living or dead,
events, or locales is entirely coincidental.

Print information available on the last page

Rev. date: 03/22/2016

To order additional copies of this book, contact:
Xlibris
1-888-795-4274
www.Xlibris.com
Orders@Xlibris.com

INTRODUCTION

The Bible tell us as Godly parents that we should **"Train up a child in the way he should go, and when he is old, he will not depart from it."** *Proverbs 22:6*

Another translation says "Train up a child in the way he should go [teaching him to seek God's wisdom and will for his abilities and talents}, Even when he is old he will not depart from it." So as Godly parents we should naturally teach and instruct our children God's way, his will for their life and how to be good stewards of their God-given talents and abilities. I'm writing this resource guide to help parents teach their child at an early age how to build lasting wealth from a Christian perspective. When I was a kid, I was poor and grew up in the projects. Always fantasizing I was rich and a child of a King that lived in a mansion high on a hill and that my God supplied all my needs. I dreamed of living a wonderful plush lifestyle and one day I would grow up to be a King, just like King Solomon in the Bible

1 Kings 3:3-11. The Bible tells us of the Lord making Solomon wise. Solomon loved the Lord and walked in the statutes of David, his father: The Lord appeared to Solomon in a dream saying, ask what I shall give Thee? Solomon asked for wisdom-"an understanding heart!"- To lead well and make right decisions, God gave him wisdom, wealth and a long life to lead his chosen people, and that should be our prayer to God as well. Give us the wisdom to know what to do with the resources he gives us. God does not promise riches to those who follow him, but he gives us what we need if we put his Kingdom and his interests first. **Matthew 6:31-33**

In this resource guide, your child will learn the three basic principles on how to build lasting wealth from a Christian perspective, in a simple and systematic way. Saving, spending and investing. When we plan for the future, it is time well spent, when we worry about tomorrow, it's time wasted. So let's jump in and get started!

Train up a child in the way he should go, and when he is old, he will not depart from it. *Proverbs 22:6*

DISCIPLINE

Ecclesiastes 3:9,12 and 13

⁹What profit has the worker from that in which he labors?

¹² I know that nothing is better for them than to rejoice, and to do good in their lives, ¹³ and also that every man should eat and drink and enjoy the good of all his labor—it is the gift of God.

Training and Discipline

Although raking leaves is a simple task, it also teaches a child discipline and responsibility.

SPENDING

I'm learning to share. Grandmommy tells me it builds character and values.

SPENDING

1 Samuel 18: 3, 4 [3] *Then Jonathan and David made a covenant because he loved him as his own soul.* [4] *And Jonathan took off the robe that was on him and gave it to David, with his armor, even to his sword and his bow and his belt.*

Grandmommy taught me at an early age that it is alright to share my success with others, but we should always base our friendships on our commitment to God, not just to each other. Sharing what we have with others shows generosity and true friendship.

TITHING

Malachi 3:10

^{10} *Bring all the tithes into the storehouse that there may be food in My house, And try Me now in this," Says the Lord of hosts, "If I will not open for you the windows of heaven And pour out for you such blessing That there will not be room enough to receive it.*

INVESTING

Matthew 5:16

[16] *Let your light so shine before men that they may see your good works and glorify your Father, which is in heaven.*

INVESTING

Playing with fun stuff like hot wheels, comic books, gaming systems or even learning to play an instrument can be a gateway to investing, building character and creating a good value system.

INVESTING

Matthew 25:20-30

The story of the 5, 2 and one talent teaches children the power of investing.

[20]"So he who had received five talents came and brought five other talents, saying, 'Lord, you delivered to me five talents; look, I have gained five more talents besides them.' [21] His lord said to him, 'Well done, good and faithful servant; you were faithful over a few things, I will make you ruler over many things. Enter into the joy of your lord.' [22] He also who had received two talents came and said, 'Lord, you delivered to me two talents; look, I have gained two more talents besides them.' [23] His lord said to him, 'Well done, good and faithful servant; you have been faithful over a few things, I will make you ruler over many things. Enter into the joy of your lord.'

Buying coins is a great hobby, and it's profitable too. Investing is so rewarding when you see your money grow!

SAVING

Whatever your passion, try to figure out a way to make it profitable!!

Being creative with our God-given gifts and talents can be very rewarding and generate great success. We must always give God the glory and be good stewards over what we have.

TEACHABLE MOMENTS

Train up a child in the way he should go, and when he is old, he will not depart from it. **Proverbs 22:6**

Another translation says, "Train up a child in the way he should go [teaching him to seek God's wisdom and will for his abilities and talents], Even when he is old he will not depart from it."

So as Godly parents we should naturally train, teach and instruct our children God's way, his will for their life and how to be good stewards of their God-given talents and abilities. Constantly reminding our children the real pleasure is found not in what we accumulate, but in enjoying whatever we have as gifts from God.

VOCABULARY WORDS

Discipline : to train (yourself) to do something by controlling your behavior

Save: to put aside money or to spend less money

Spend: to use (money) to pay for something

Invest: to grant someone control or authority over money in order to earn a financial return

Coins: a usually flat piece of metal issued by governmental authority as money

Usury: The practice of lending money and requiring the borrower to pay back the amount with interest

Stewardship: the careful and responsible management of something entrusted to one's care

Gift: a special ability, a talent or something given as a present

Talent: the natural abilities of a person, a special often athletic, creative, or artistic ability or a unit of value equal to the value of a talent of gold or silver

Destiny: what happens in the future: the things that someone or something will experience in the future

Note: This vocabulary word list can be used for a Spelling test.

Destiny Word Search

```
                              S
                              E
                              R
                          M   Z   L
                          P   G   T
                          D   K   Z
                      S   T   A   W   E
                      K   E   G   C   T
                      P   K   X   S   Q
                  A   G   W   E   D   H   E
                  Y   W   V   Z   V   R   G
                  P   N   W   X   K   S   A
              W   I   C   E   R   U   X   M   M
              O   T   L   D   L   F   U   J   S
              R   U   D   L   E   A   V   B   A
K T O H U L T D V G B A T B P G G J N T O E V A S M M C R L Z T Q Q P H Q A D
O I M B D B P G N S Y H G X M O S U N D Q J S M W N A H J Y G G Q G D L B
L O J O B A N O B P E Y Z F S E H O O A R M U W E P H N D L N Q E
B A D U S U R Y X K S K G O S R P B G M L A X A R U S Y G S M
R D I R T G F E M G I Y S Z Q B O J J O T B I K I F I P N
Z O C I F N X S P I H S D R A W E T S Q F W D C H
J P F A I J N G Z X M B D F C K A P E J V K X
E T A L B I N Z F C S E C T W E E M X L V
W P E O G M Y C Q D T O P M C X R
I U C E T D G S A K W B I N I
C V E B T Y U L U W N G M C I
S F W J A P E E Y A F U W Y R
I P O L X N B L Z N N D T F R
H D T M O T J Q Y M A A F D H V Y
E S L X M K C V F L D F B R S Y Z
A U W D X S N Y H W G R U H P S Z
Y G V A F P R C B   Q X R D H E X W X
N I Z R E U E       G W D M N I B H
I O H Z Q N         X V D N I R
K T Z P A G         X U O G R U
V S U B E           I Q Z N X
L E W               L M N
G G D               X U R
N K                 V Q R
M                       R
```

WORD LIST:

COINS	GIFT	SPEND	USURY
DESTINY	INVEST	STEWARDSHIP	
DISCIPLINE	SAVE	TALENT	

14

MAZE Activity

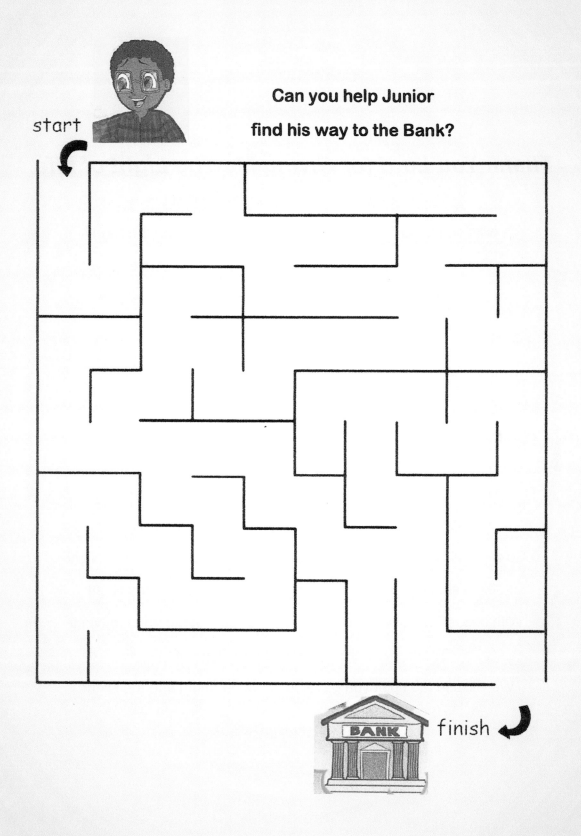

Can you help Junior find his way to the Bank?

start

finish

Thank You Lord for Giving Me The Light of Life

Thank you Lord for giving me the light of Life

I will use the spirit you gave me, to shine bright into the Night!

God spoke into darkness, and on earth he created Light

Then created man in his image, by giving him eternal Life

God created the land and, all of the tall trees

Then he created the air, that we all breathe

God created the animals, the birds and the bees

Then he created the fish of, the deep blue seas

Thank you Lord for giving me the light of Life

I will use the spirit you gave me, to shine bright into the Night!

God sent his only son and, his son gave up his life

So we could use the spirit he gave us, to shine bright into the Night

Like a shining star that's shining, shining bright into the Night

With Jesus Christ living within us, our light will overcome the Night

Thank you Lord for giving us the light of Life

We will use the spirit you gave us, to shine bright into the Night!

God's Creation

God's Ross Haynes Jr.
Creation:

Across

3 Synonym for made or invented

5 The opposite of off

6 3 letter word that rhymes with hand

8 Another word for the past tense of talk

9 4 letter word describing putting my tablet _ _ _ _ my backpack

10 The planet we live on

Down

1 Take the "s" off of she

2 The almighty

4 The absence of light

7 The opposite of dark

Thank You Lord

God spoke into darkness, and on earth he created Light

Then God created man in his image, by giving him the light of Life

Thank you, Lord, for giving me the light of Life

I will use the spirit you gave me, to shine bright into the Night!

Thank You Lord Unscramble Word Activity

1. ksoep   __ __ __ __ __

2. thbrig   __ __ __ __ __ __

3. irpist   __ __ __ __ __ __

4. emagi   __ __ __ __ __

5. shien   __ __ __ __ __

6. htlgi   __ __ __ __ __

7. Lrdo   __ __ __ __

8. nakth   __ __ __ __ __

9. uyo   __ __ __

10. ifel   __ __ __ __

SAVINGS

NOTE: Coloring page may require special coloring utensils.

20

ANSWER KEYS

Destiny Word Search

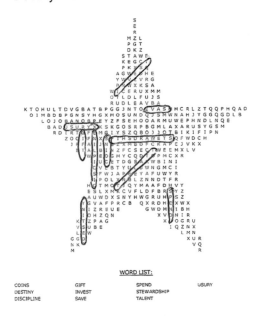

WORD LIST:

COINS	GIFT	SPEND	USURY
DESTINY	INVEST	STEWARDSHIP	
DISCIPLINE	SAVE	TALENT	

Help Junior find his way to the bank.

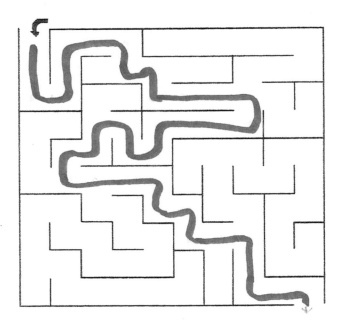

God's Creation

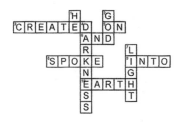

Across

3 Synonym for made or invented
5 The opposite of off
6 3 letter word that rhymes with hand
8 Another word for the past tense of talk
9 4 letter word describing putting my tablet _ _ _ _ my backpack
10 The planet we live on

Down

1 Take the "s" off of she
2 The almighty
4 The absence of light
7 The opposite of dark

Thank You Lord Unscramble Word Activity

1. Ksoep   S P O K E
2. Thbrig   B R I G H T
3. Irpist   S P I R I T
4. Emagi   I M A G E
5. Shien   S H I N E
6. Htlgi   L I G H T
7. Lrdo   L O R D
8. Nakth   T H A N K
9. uyo   Y O U
10. ifel   L I F E

Printed in the United States
By Bookmasters